Walking to Corroboree

Written and illustrated by

Anne Kerr & Rhanee Tsetsakos

Published by Boolarong Press,
655 Toohey Road
Salisbury Qld 4107
Australia.
www.boolarongpress.com.au

First published 2018

A catalogue record for this book is available from the National Library of Australia

ISBN: 9781925522747

Cover artwork by Teenie Wilton

The artwork is a collage of scenes that depicts how it was back in traditional days for the people of the land. The child peeping over the bush and looking at the butterfly represents happiness and complete freedom, as does the children swimming in the water. The colours of the Butterfly represents the soulful connection between the people and the land. Water represents purity. To our children and to our Elders, this was, and still is, paradise.

Printed and bound by Watson Ferguson & Company, Salisbury, Australia

The language used in this book comes from the Adnyamathanha people who originate from the Northern Flinders Ranges in South Australia. Their language is one of the few Aboriginal languages still spoken today. This can be incorporated incrementally as the reader's confidence grows.

Pronounced:

"udd-n-ya-muth-a-na" - Adnyamathanha

This is a story of Australia's History.
It is a true story.

In the old, old, old days the bushland was thick and strong. The creeks and rivers were full and would flow where they wanted, down into the sea. Mobs of udlu (kangaroos) nibbled at the tall grass and clouds of birds filled the sky.

Pronounced:
"ood-loo" - kangaroo

The First Australians walked softly on the land. This was Adnyamathanha yata (country). Running amongst them were the yakatis (children) laughing and playing. The yakatis (children) knew that today was a walking day and that they would be tired by nightfall.

Pronounced:

"udd-n-ya-muth-a-na" - Adnyamathnha

"yar-ta" - country

"yuk-ar-tees" - children

Before the yundu (sun) went down the yakatis (children) would help the grown-ups and the older children collect sticks and branches for the adla (fire) they would have that night.

Pronounced
"yoon-doo" - sun
"ud-lar" - fire
"yuk-ar-tees" - children

They would curl up in front of the adla (fire) and watch the sparks dance up to the stars. They would listen to the elders tell stories of their ancestors, of the animals and birds and then fall happily asleep.

Pronounced:
"ud-lar" - fire

If it was cold their mums and aunties would cover them with a warm **udlu** (kangaroo) or possum fur. If it rained they would build a shelter of branches and leaves. The **wadli** (shelter) was **wandu** (good) and strong and would keep them safe throughout the night.

Pronounced:

"ood-loo" - kangaroo

"wod-lee" - shelter

"won-doo" - good

Tomorrow, was going to be another long day. The yakatis (children) helped to pick berries, nuts and seeds from plants and bushes. They dug deep into the ground and looked in the tree trunks for yams, honey ants and witati (witchetty grub).

Pronounced:

"yuk-ar-tees"- children

"witch-a-tee" - witchetty grub

The land was their mita (friend) and it looked after them. In return, they respected and cared for it and took only what they needed.

Pronounced:
"mit-a" - friend

Their fathers and uncles would take the younger men hunting, carrying their shields, woomeras, wadnas (boomerangs) and wadlatas (spears). They would watch the land as they walked reading the signs that it gave them. Broken branches, tracks of udlu (kangaroo), warrati (emu) or goanna. The young men would learn from their elders by following these signs and maybe spear an udlu (kangaroo) or two to cook in the adla (fire) to share.

Pronounced:

"wod-nas" - boomerangs

"wod-lar-thas" - spears

"wod-ar-chee" - emu

"ood-loo" - kangaroo

"ud-lar" - fire

The yakatis (children) would watch the older kids and try to copy them. They would pretend to follow tracks and search for each other in the long grass.

Pronounced:
"yuk-ar-tees" -children

The yakatis (children) could tell that this walking trip was a special one. They heard the elders talking quietly together each night carefully planning the next day. They could see their mums, aunties and grandmas were eager to get to their destination.

Pronounced:
"yuk-ar-tees" - children

The yakatis (children) were curious. "What's going on?" they asked, "Where are we going?"

Adnani (grandma) would say, "Shh, shh, shh wadikana yakatis." "Wait and see children, wait and see".

But it was hard.....soo hard to wait for sooooo long.

Adnani (grandma) gave them an important job to do.

"You grab that viti (carrying dish) and let's go collect berries to snack on as we walk today"

Pronounced:

"yuk-ar-tees" - children

"ud-nya-nee" - grandma

"wodee-ka-nay" - wait

"vitch-ee" - carrying dish

After another day of walking the family rested.
The yakatis (children) could see the vundu (smoke) from many campfires in the distance.

Pronounced:
"yuk-ar-tees" - children
"voon-doo" - smoke

Adnani (grandma) took their hands and gestured to the campfires. "Yakatis (children), we are nearly there. It is not far to walk now." Adnani (grandma) told them of all the wonderful things that waited for them and said, "You will meet lots of new people, you will hear many different stories and you will see lots of new things."

Pronounced:

"udd-n-ya-nee" - grandma

"yuk-ar-tees" - children

Finally, they had arrived and the yakatis were exhausted. But Adnani (grandma) was right! As the crowds of friendly faces happily welcomed them they could feel the excitement in the air. It was time for a celebration!

Pronounced:

"yuk-ar-tees" - children

"udd-n-ya-nee" - grandma

Adnani (grandma) explained that each night the families would come together to eat, sing, and dance.
She said, "The Adnyamathanha people have been gathering here for a long, long time. This is a very special meeting place. This is uri mutandana (Corroboree)"

Pronounced:
"udd-n-ya-nee" - grandma
"udd-n-ya-muth-a-na" - Adnyamathanha
"oo-di mut-an-dana" - corroboree

As the yakatis (children) went to miya (sleep) around the big adla (campfire) their wallas (bellies) were full and their hearts were happy. Yes, indeed this was a SPECIAL walk, and this was a SPECIAL place. They would always remember this journey of walking to Corroboree.

Pronounced:
"yuk-ar-tees" - children
"mee-ah" - sleep
"ud-lar" - fire
"wul-ars" - bellies

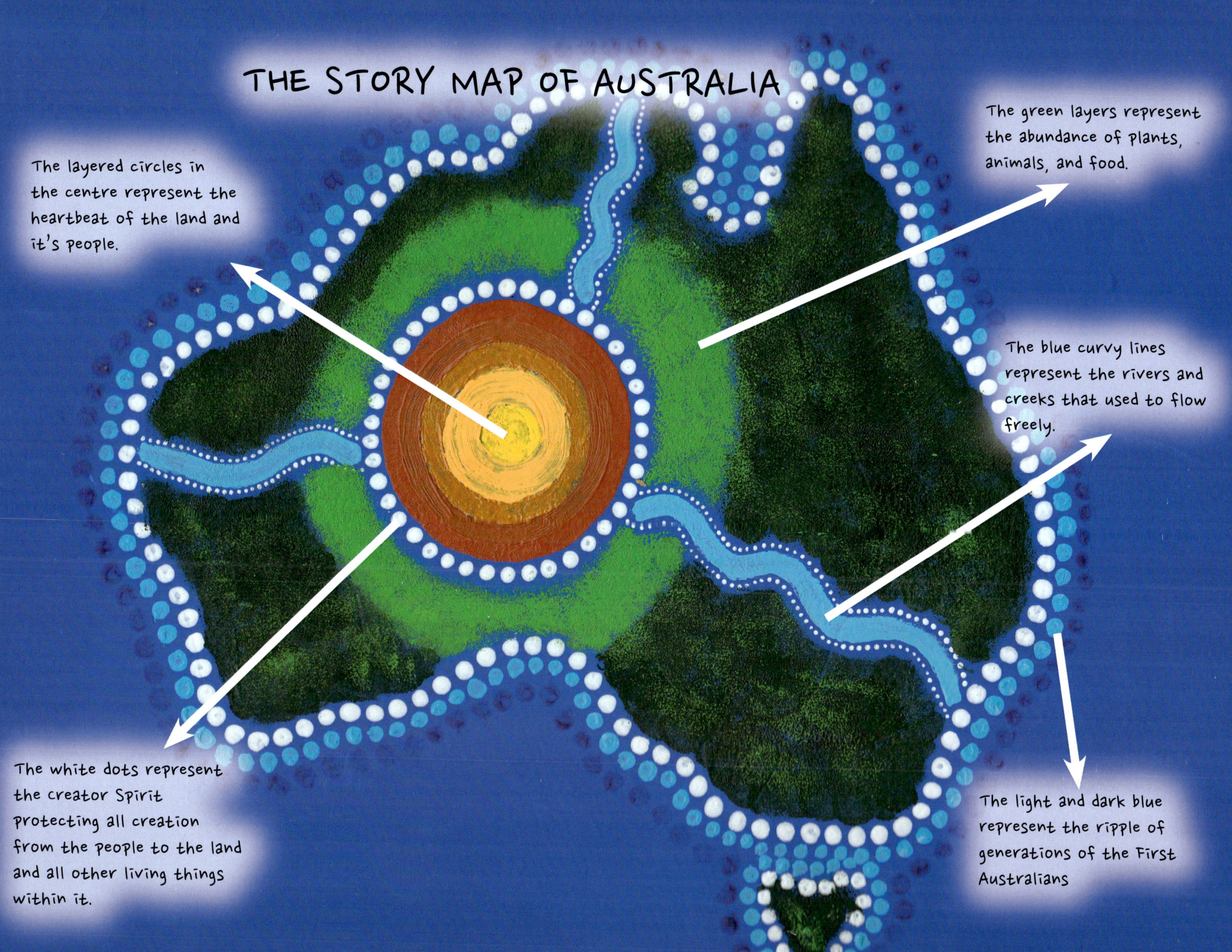
THE STORY MAP OF AUSTRALIA
The layered circles in the centre represent the heartbeat of the land and it's people.
The green layers represent the abundance of plants, animals, and food.
The blue curvy lines represent the rivers and creeks that used to flow freely.
The white dots represent the creator Spirit protecting all creation from the people to the land and all other living things within it.
The light and dark blue represent the ripple of generations of the First Australians

HOW TO USE THIS BOOK:

The aim of this book is to introduce the true history of Australia and its First People's to young children who are at the beginning of their educational journey. We want to create a culture of respect and awareness in our young ones, about the role our First People's played in caring for Australia before "The Others" arrived. This book will give young children an appreciation of how the First Australians were connected to the land and how both sustained each other for more than 60,000 years. We hope that this book will open a door to people's minds about what life was like for an Aboriginal family before the arrival of settlers, so that people have a better understanding of Aboriginal culture and the importance of their connection to country. This book is to be used as a helpful tool for all peoples, to initiate conversations about Aboriginal culture and to establish positive connections and relationships with Aboriginal people and their communities.

Positive Messages:

- Acknowledgement of country. Staying together and looking out for the little ones. Duty of care (p. 2)
- Helping each other. Many hands make light work (p. 3)
- Learning from each other by talking and listening carefully (p. 4)
- Feeling safe, warm and loved (p. 5)
- caring for the environment, sustainability (p. 6 & 8)
- Eating healthy food (p. 6)
- Strong role models, reading the signs, tracking (p. 10)
- Being creative, using your imagination, making friends. Safe play (p. 12)
- Having a plan (p. 13)
- Patience, self-worth. Being part of a team (p. 14)

- knowing when to rest (p. 16)
- Preparing yourself for what's ahead, expectations, variety (p. 18)
- Arriving at your destination, building relationships, being inclusive, hospitality, community (p. 20)
- Learning about cultures, belonging, celebration, new season, respecting other's cultures (p. 22)
- Healthy mind, healthy body, healthy heart, healthy spirit (Pg.24)

challenges

1. Find out what the name is of the traditional owners/language group in your area?
2. Develop a 'Reconciliation Action Plan' also known as a RAP for your classroom.
3. Invite an Aboriginal Elder to your classroom to share a story.
4. Learn some words in an Aboriginal Language from your area.
5. Learn about a Dreamtime Story from a significant site in your area.
6. YouTube a Corroboree. Put on a class Corroboree. Research the rituals that were observed.
7. YouTube digging for honey ants, finding water, bush tucker.

comparable Bridge of understanding:

What is a Corroboree? Corroboree is a gathering together of many language groups for the purpose of exchanging ideas, tools, songs, musical instruments and food. It is a community gathering where relationships are renewed and news is exchanged. Think of a modern day gathering. When families get together for Christmas each year is this similar to Corroboree? In what way? What traditions does your family observe at Christmas time? can you see how the Corroboree celebration and the Christmas celebration are similar? Does your family go to church, travel to be together with aunties, uncles, grandparents and friends? Is there special food? Is there music and laughter, fun and games? Do you catch up on all the family news. Do you gather around the Christmas tree?

About the Authors

Anne Kerr is a Kindergarten Educator of 28 years' experience relating to children aged 3-5 years. She knows how important reading and telling stories are to this age group in helping them understand and make sense of their world.

"Walking to Corroboree" was a collaborative project with Rhanee Tsetsakos, an Adnyamathanha woman from South Australia. Discussing and painting the book together represents reconciliation in action.

"Walking to Corroboree" is a gentle book that tells the story of an Aboriginal family group walking in community and harmony as they move at one with the land - finding food and shelter along the way. There is respect and gratitude to country and mounting excitement and anticipation as the family moves softly across the different Australian landscapes until finally reaching their destination - Corroboree!

Young children will enjoy the eye-catching illustrations and learn to appreciate how the land and the people can co-exist together. It is a privilege that the language of Rhanee's people, the Adnyamathanha, is embedded for use throughout the story. Many thanks for this opportunity.

RHANEE TSETSAKOS grew up in a country town called Port Augusta, in South Australia. Her Aboriginal ancestry is tied to her mother's people, the Adnyamathanha of the Northern Flinders Ranges, South Australia. Rhanee also embraces her father's side which is a mixture of English and Indian, making her family a melting pot of different cultures. She enjoys using her imagination and being creative and very much loved English and Art subjects at school. She has a deep passion for constantly learning about her culture, and although she is not a fluent speaker of the Adnyamathanha language, she feels that by working on projects like the "Walking to Corroboree" book, will help her in her goal to understanding and speaking more of her language. The language used in this book was passed down to Rhanee from her Auntie Pauline McKenzie, with the use of the ADNA-MAT-NA Dictionary which was put together by Rhanee's Nanna Pearl McKenzie.

Cover Artist's Profile

Teenie Wilton is an "Ugarapul/Gungarri" woman on her Father's side, "Koombumerri" and "Batjala/Kabi Kabi" on her Mother's side. She was born in Beaudesert, Queensland.

She began painting at the age of six, following in the footsteps of her elder sister Marcia who was her inspiration. She spent her childhood, along with her siblings, at The Hollow, Beaudesert, Queensland, being taught the traditional laws of the land by her parents, grandparents, aunties and uncles. They were told stories about their traditional ancestors and how they interacted with the land, the birds and the animals and thc laws that governed them in those days. She and her siblings, still continue to pass those laws down to their children and grandchildren today educating them in the way that they were. The most important law that their parents quite often emphasized was the law of respect for the land and everything it held. It was very important as the land was the lifeline of their ancestors and so it is for them today. To help keep these laws alive she has taken the stories and transformed them into pieces of artwork, writing an explanation of each to educate the buyer and anyone who happens to see her work. Photos are taken of every artwork with the intention that one day in the near future a book will be produced that explains both the picture, the law attached and where it fits into traditional aboriginal culture.

Her heart goes into every painting that she does. It is that which brings alive her love for her culture, her people and her land.